The Mystery of the Maize

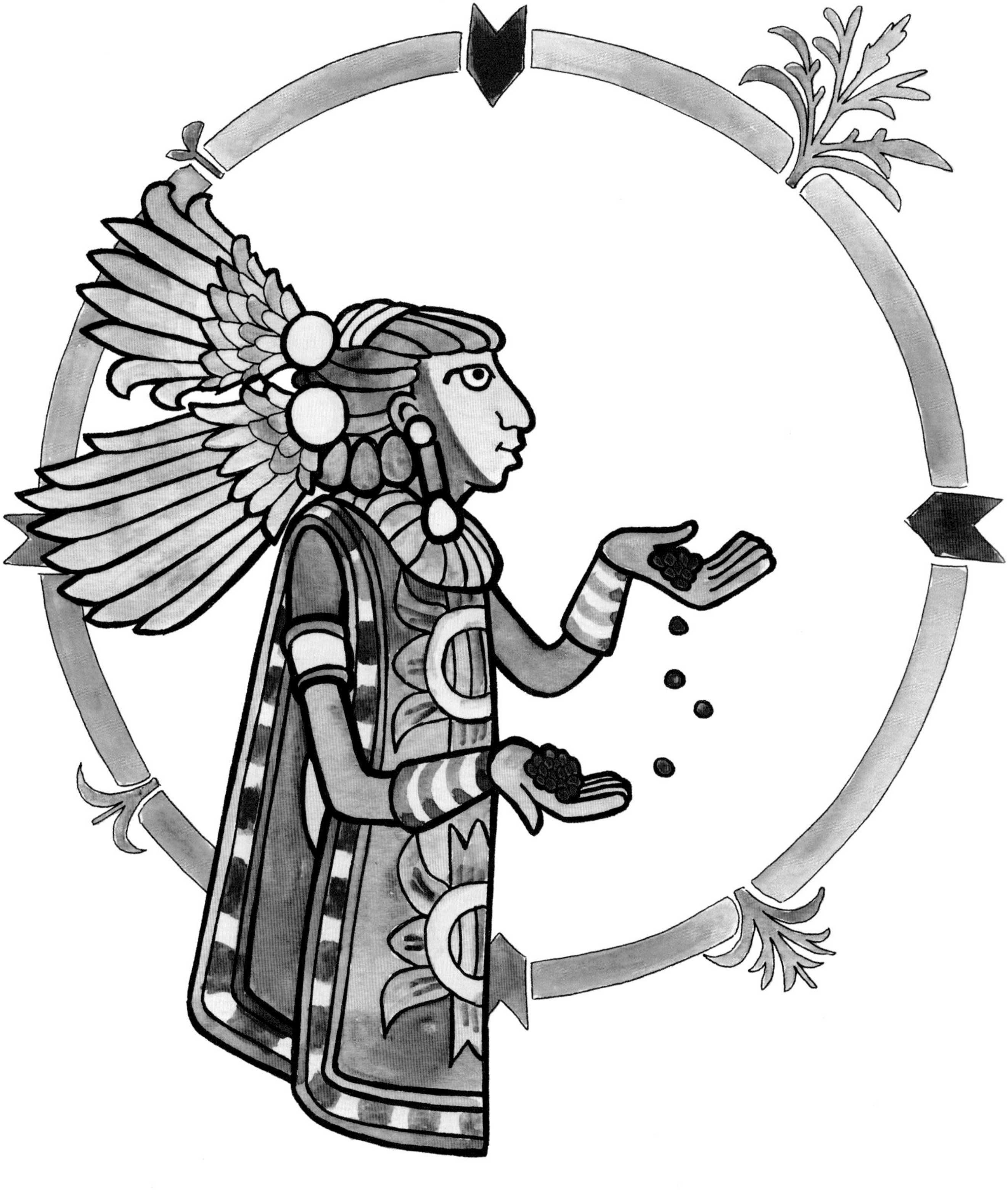

The
Mystery of the
Maize

by MARK MEIERHENRY and DAVID VOLK

Illustrated by MARTY TWO BULLS, SR.

SOUTH DAKOTA STATE HISTORICAL SOCIETY PRESS PIERRE

This publication was funded, in part, by the

Great Plains Education Foundation, Inc., Aberdeen, S.Dak.

Library of Congress Cataloging-in-Publication Data

Meierhenry, Mark V.

The mystery of the maize / by Mark Meierhenry and David Volk ;

illustrated by Marty Two Bulls, Sr.

p. cm.

Summary: Twins Heron and Muskrat learn about maize from their grandfather,

who gives Heron a bone carving of four people with maize plants, and a thousand years later,

Hannah finds the carving as she and her brother Max are learning about corn, or maize,

from their own grandfather.

ISBN 978-0-9822749-1-0

[1. Corn—Fiction. 2. Grandfathers—Fiction. 3. Brothers and sisters—Fiction.

4. Indians of North America—South Dakota—Fiction. 5. Corn Palace (Mitchell, S.D.)—Fiction.

6. South Dakota—Fiction. 7. South Dakota—History—To 1500—Fiction.] I. Volk, David, 1947- II.

Two Bulls, Marty Grant, 1962- ill. III. Title.

PZ7.M5149Mys 2010

[Fic]—dc22

2009037635

Manufactured by Regent Publishing Services, Hong Kong. Printed January 2010 in ShenZhen, China

14 13 12 11 10 1 2 3 4 5

This book is dedicated to those people,
both past and present, who have grown food
so that all of us can eat.

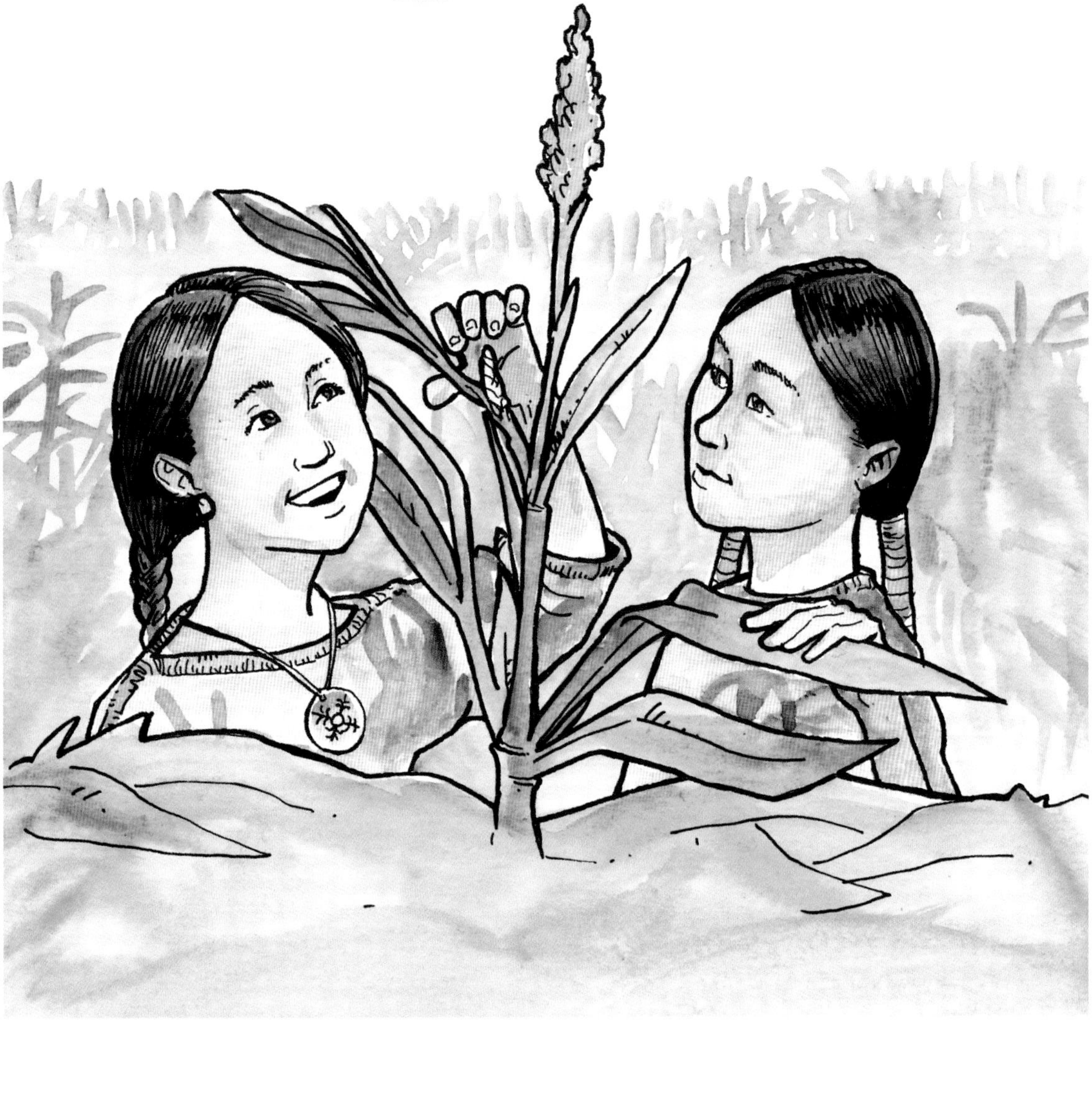

The Mystery of the Maize

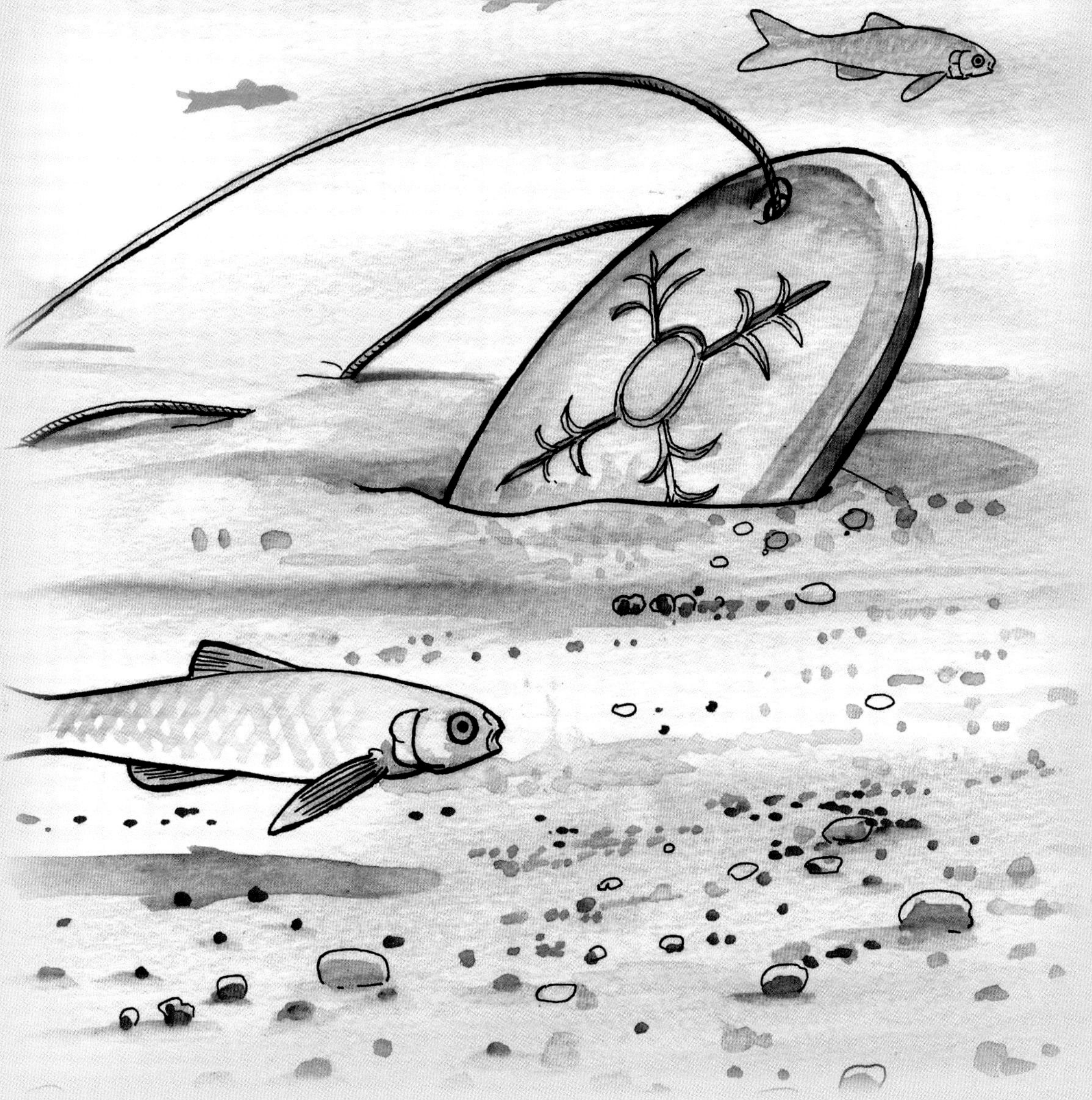

A long, long time ago . . .

Six thousand years ago, many people were visiting along a river in what is now the southern United States. A trader from the south spread colored seeds in the sunlight.

"If you put these into the ground in the spring and take care of them throughout the summer, they will grow a wonderful food," said the man who had spread the seeds before the onlookers. "The kernels of this plant can be dried and stored. It will help feed people throughout the long, cold winters. You can store it for the years when game will not come to your arrows and traps."

The people looked down at the deep red seeds sprinkled across the ground and wondered how something so small could grow into something that could feed them through the winter? They did not know yet that these tiny seeds were going to change their way of life forever.

The mystery of the maize was about to be revealed.

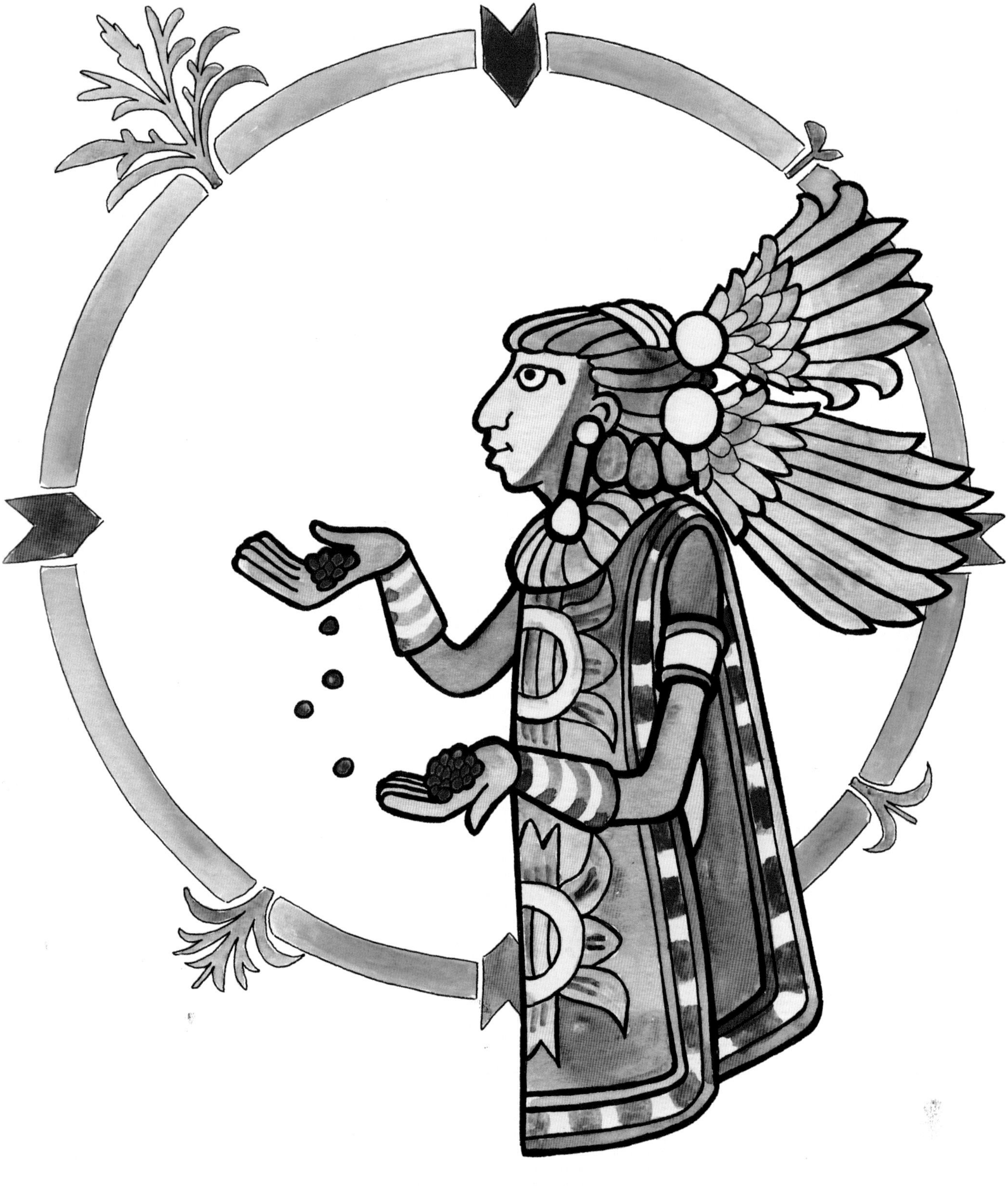

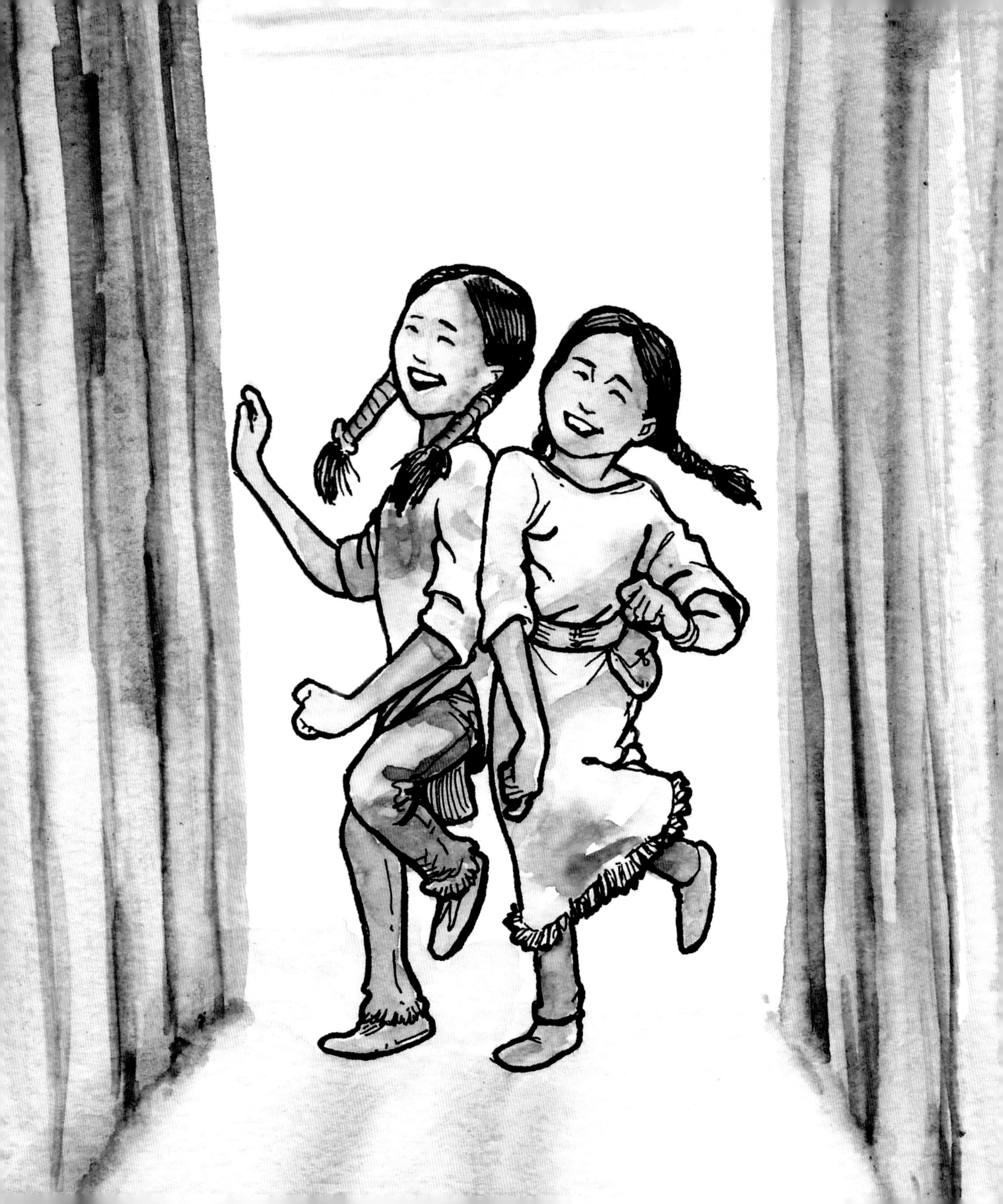

CHAPTER 1

A long time ago . . .

A thousand years ago, in a small village along
a creek running past what today is known as Mitchell,
South Dakota, Heron and her twin brother Muskrat
dressed quickly. They rushed to the opening of the
earth lodge. Arriving at the door together, they
squealed with laughter as they became stuck.

They had come into the village late the night
before from the far north and were eager to see their
grandfather, Chief White Bear. He had promised to
show them something new and exciting.

Outside, their grandmother, Silver Fox, smiled at them. "You two are not going anywhere until you have eaten," she said. The delicious smell of the rabbit stew on the open campfire made the waiting easier.

"Grandmother, what is Grandfather's secret?" asked Muskrat between bites.

Silver Fox laughed. "Muskrat, would it be a secret if I told you?"

"If you two are finished eating all of your grandmother's stew," Chief White Bear said as he came up to the edge of the campfire, "then I will show you the surprise."

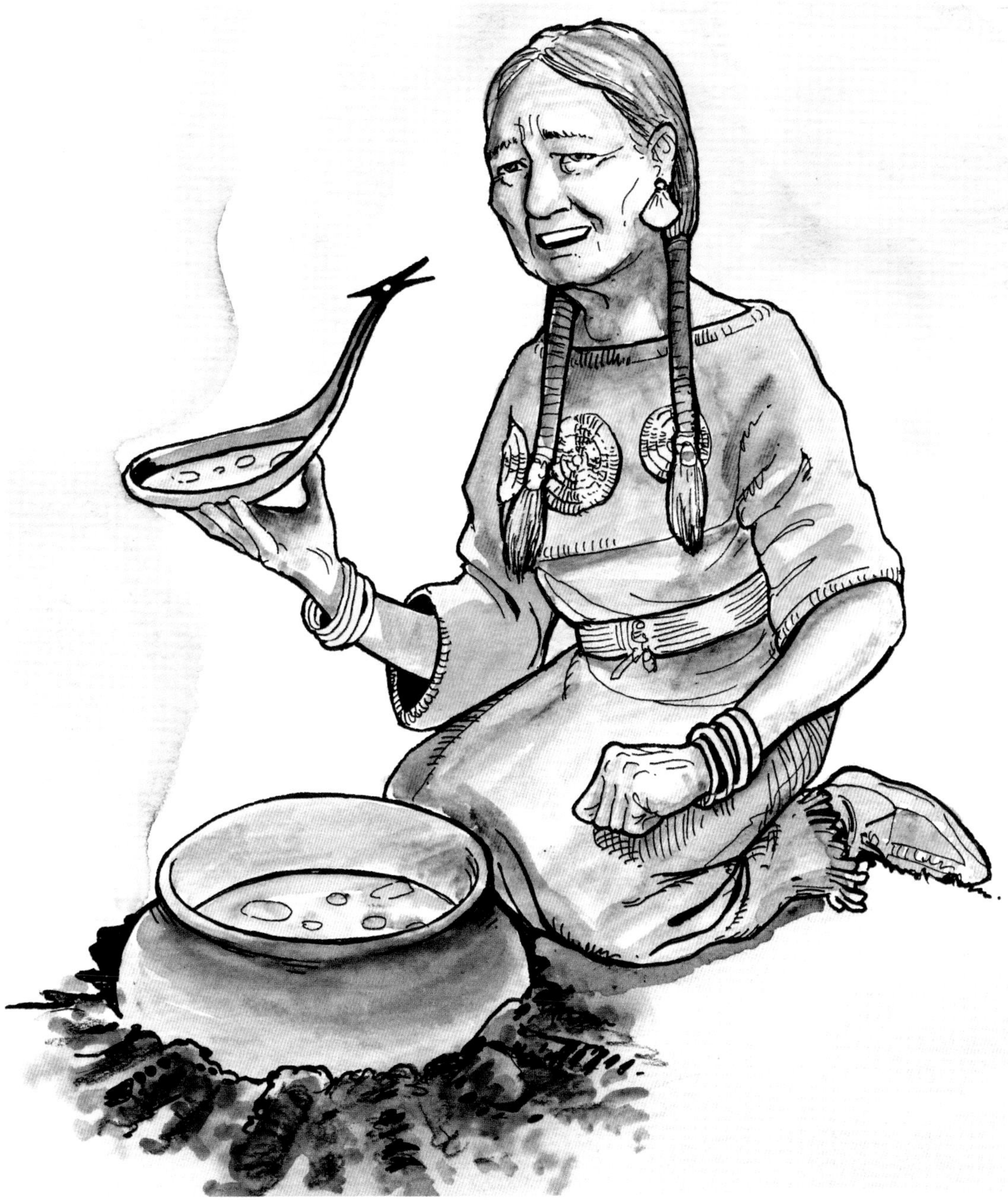

The three of them walked hand in hand through the village and down to the river bottom. There, a small field of tall plants glistened in the summer sun.

"It is called maize, and soon we will pick the ears and eat the kernels. Grandmother will dry some of it and store it in the ground. In the winter, it will help feed us, along with meat from the bison and fish from the creek."

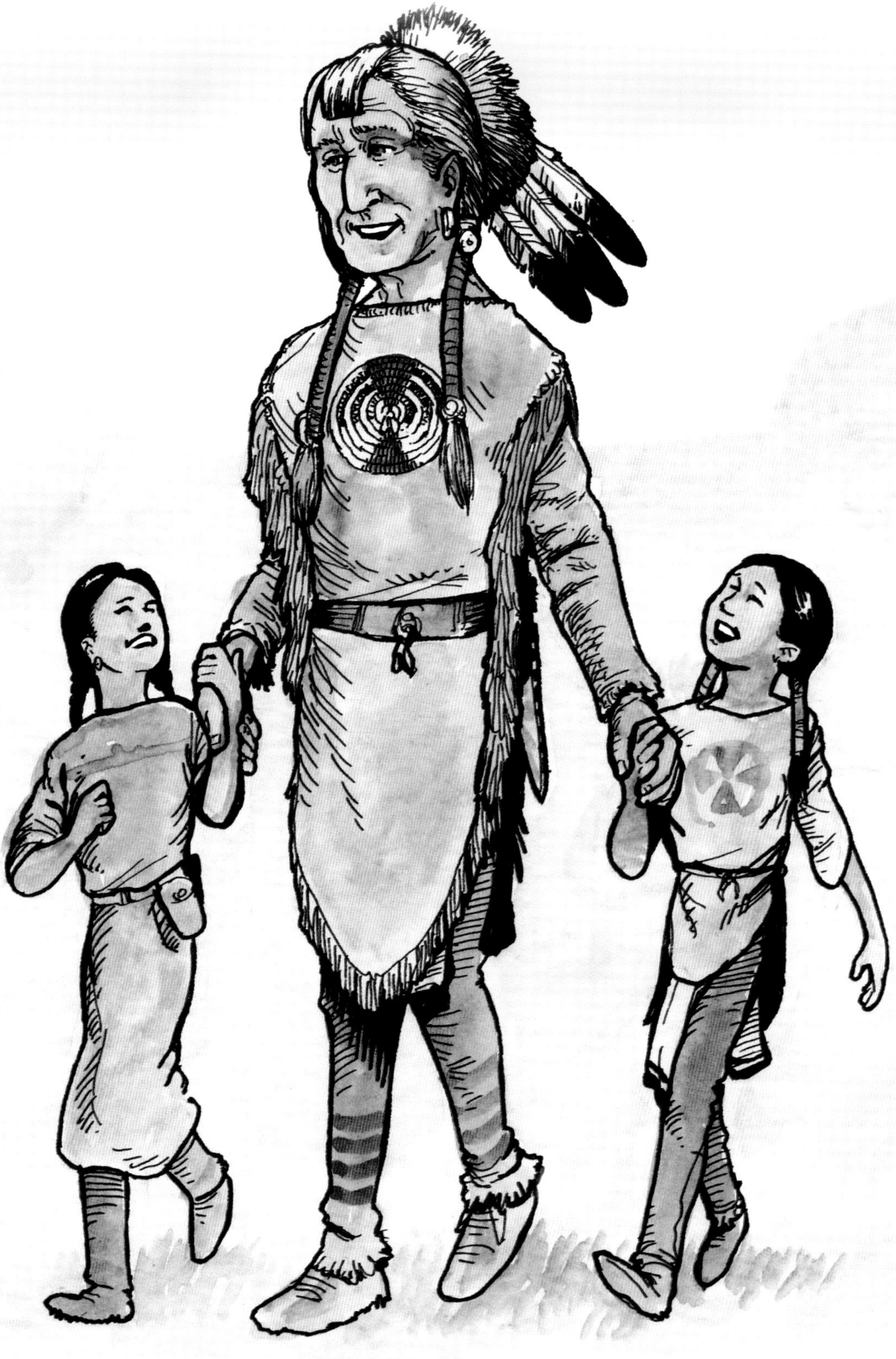

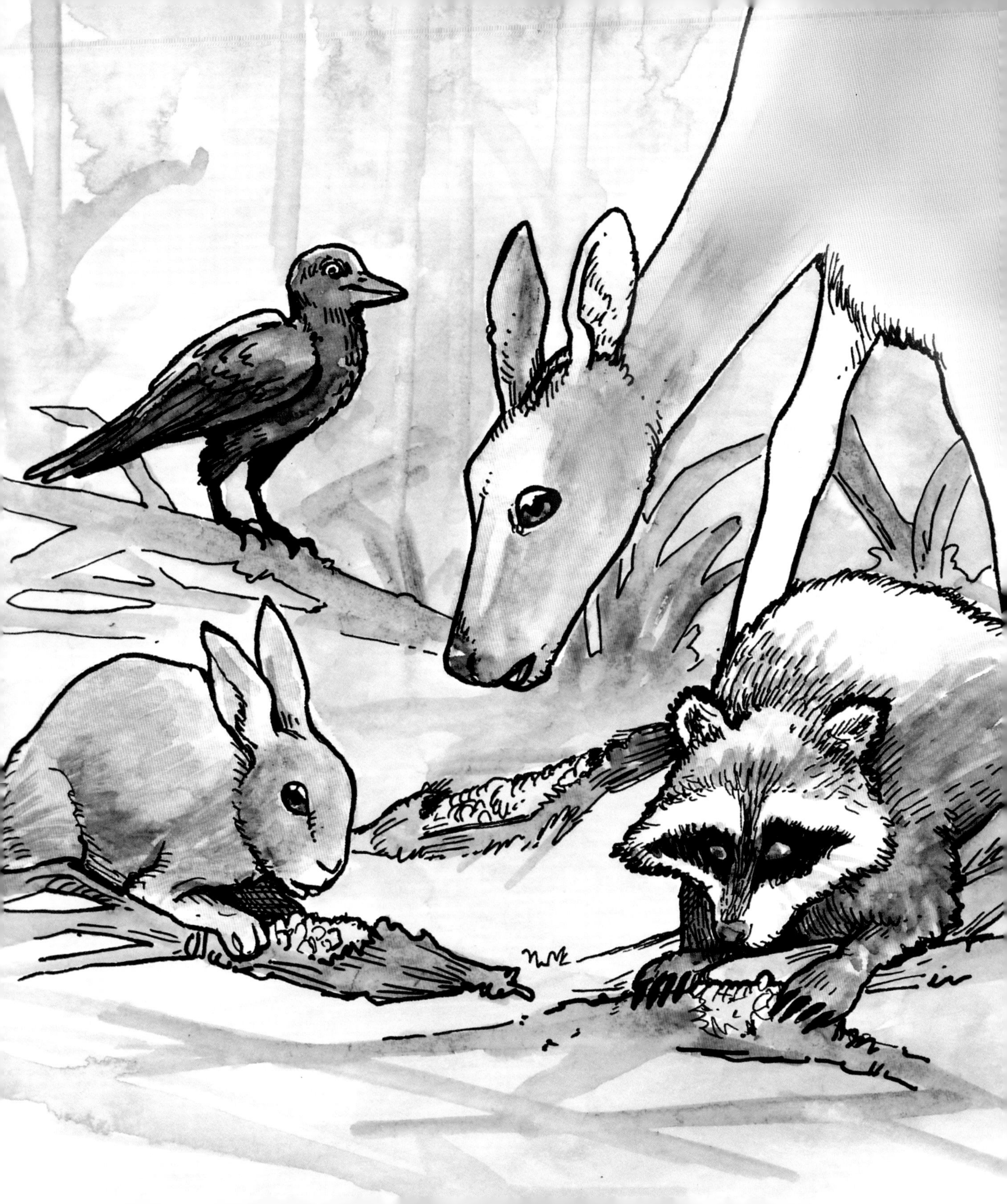

The twins marveled at the tall stalks and the ears of corn that ripened in the sun.

The maize grew throughout that long ago summer, much to the wonder of White Bear's people. The women tended the crops and soon learned that other animals liked the new food, too. Rabbits, deer, birds, and raccoons were always looking for an easy meal.

"Heron," said Grandmother, "today you will help me watch over the maize while Muskrat goes with Grandfather. We will sit in the field and sing to the plants and scare away intruders with our songs."

As Heron stood watch in the field, she fell asleep on the small platform that her grandmother had made. A rustling noise and a horrible smell awoke her. She jumped up and tumbled off the platform.

She was staring up at the biggest, ugliest bison she had ever seen. The old bull, with only one eye, had been separated from his herd, and he did not like little girls who surprised him.

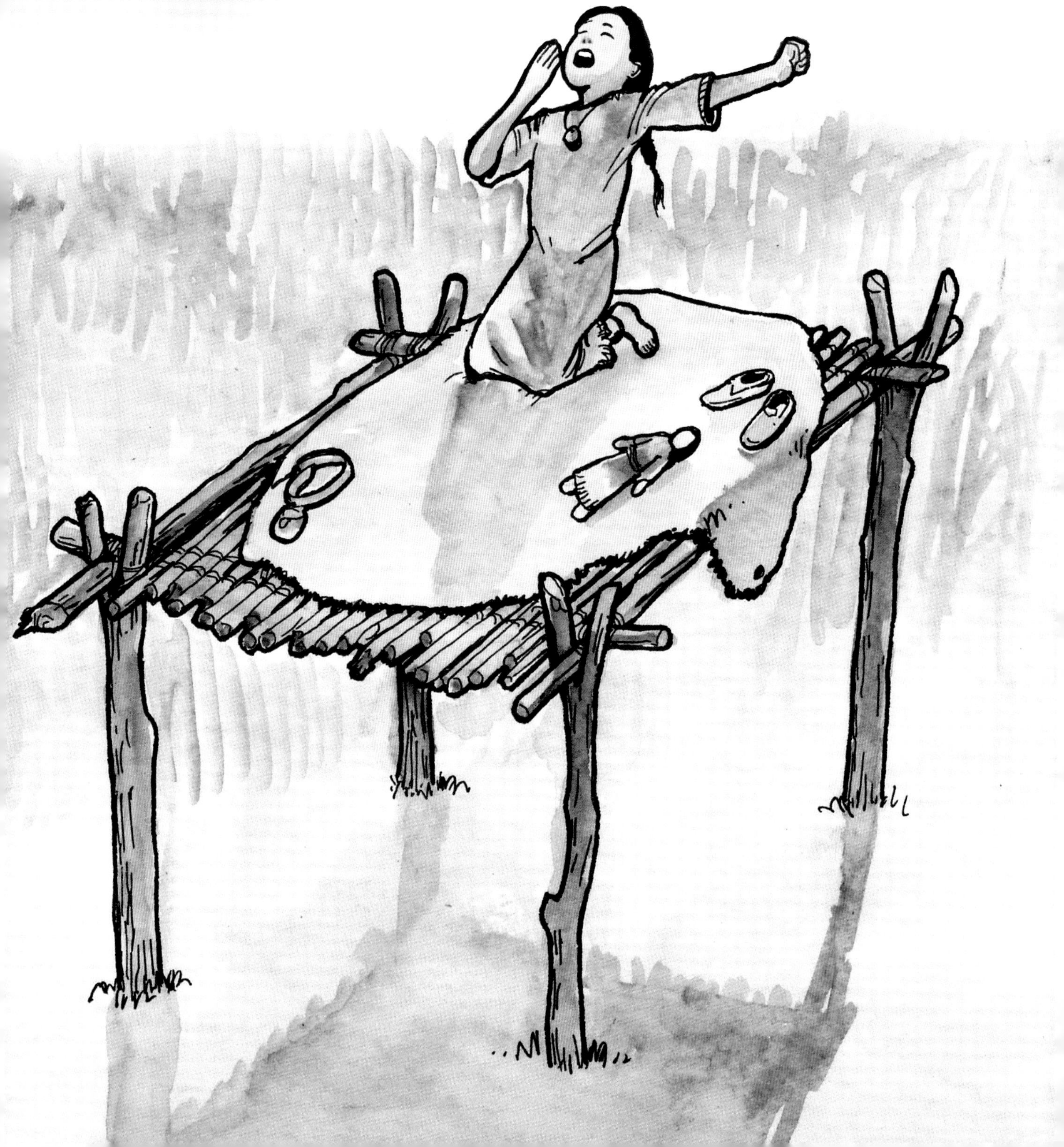

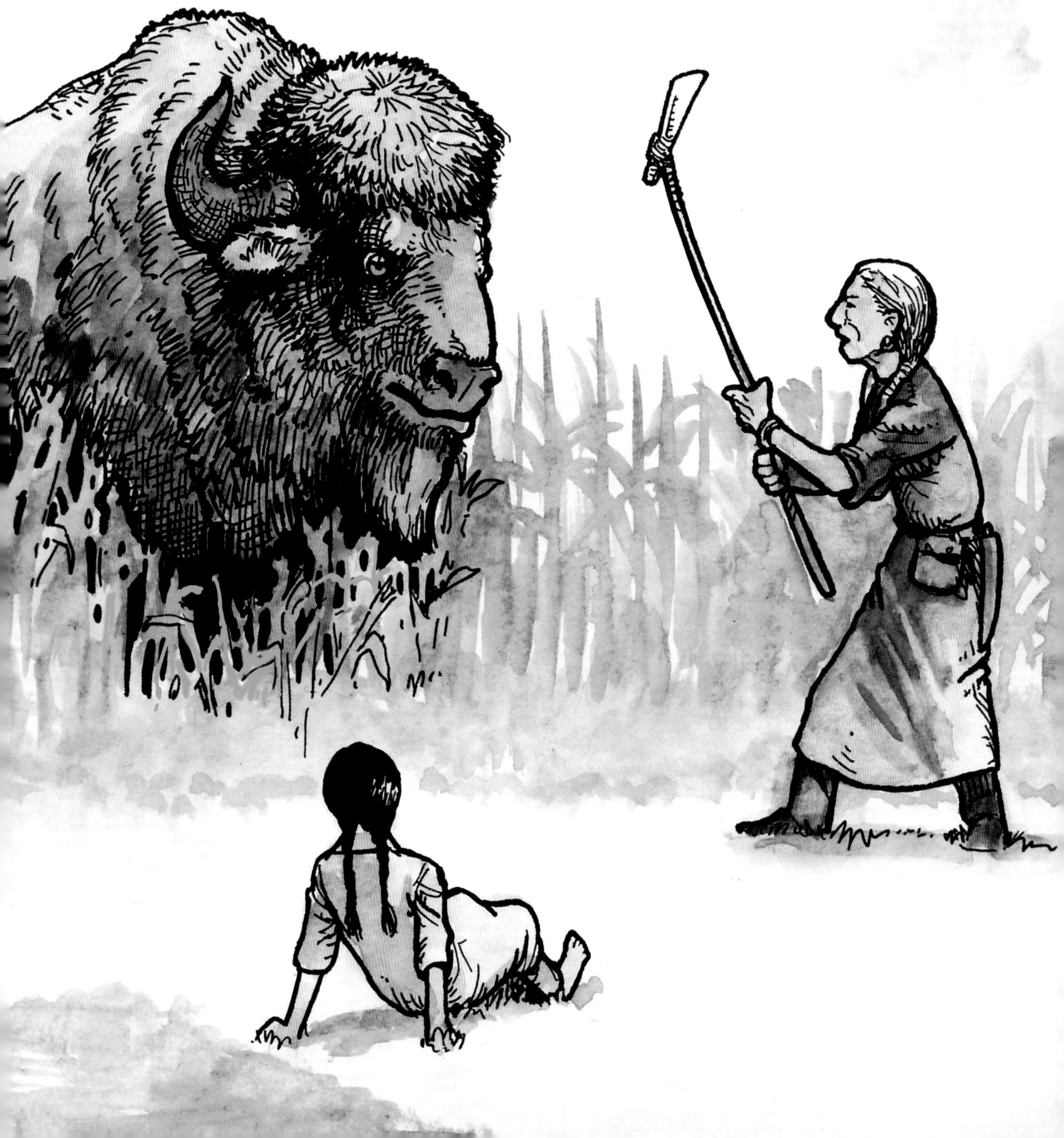

Heron closed her eyes in sudden fright as the big bull snorted and pawed the ground. Then she heard a loud *whack*.

When she opened her eyes, she was amazed to see her grandmother hitting the old bull's nose with her bone hoe. The bison shook his head in confusion. Grandmother gave him another mighty *thwack* on his nose. He quickly moved off.

Even though he was an old bison, he could still learn lessons. Today he learned not to threaten little girls when their grandmothers were nearby.

The next day, Chief White Bear found Heron sitting by herself in the lodge.

"I had a dream last night," he said. "I was told to give you this small piece of bison bone on which I have carved four maize plants. Two of the plants stand for you and your brother. They will protect you twins from harm."

"Thank you, Grandfather. But why are there four plants rather than two?" Heron asked.

"The dream did not show me the meaning of the other two plants," he said.

Grandfather had drilled a hole in the bone and put it on a leather thong so that she could wear it around her neck.

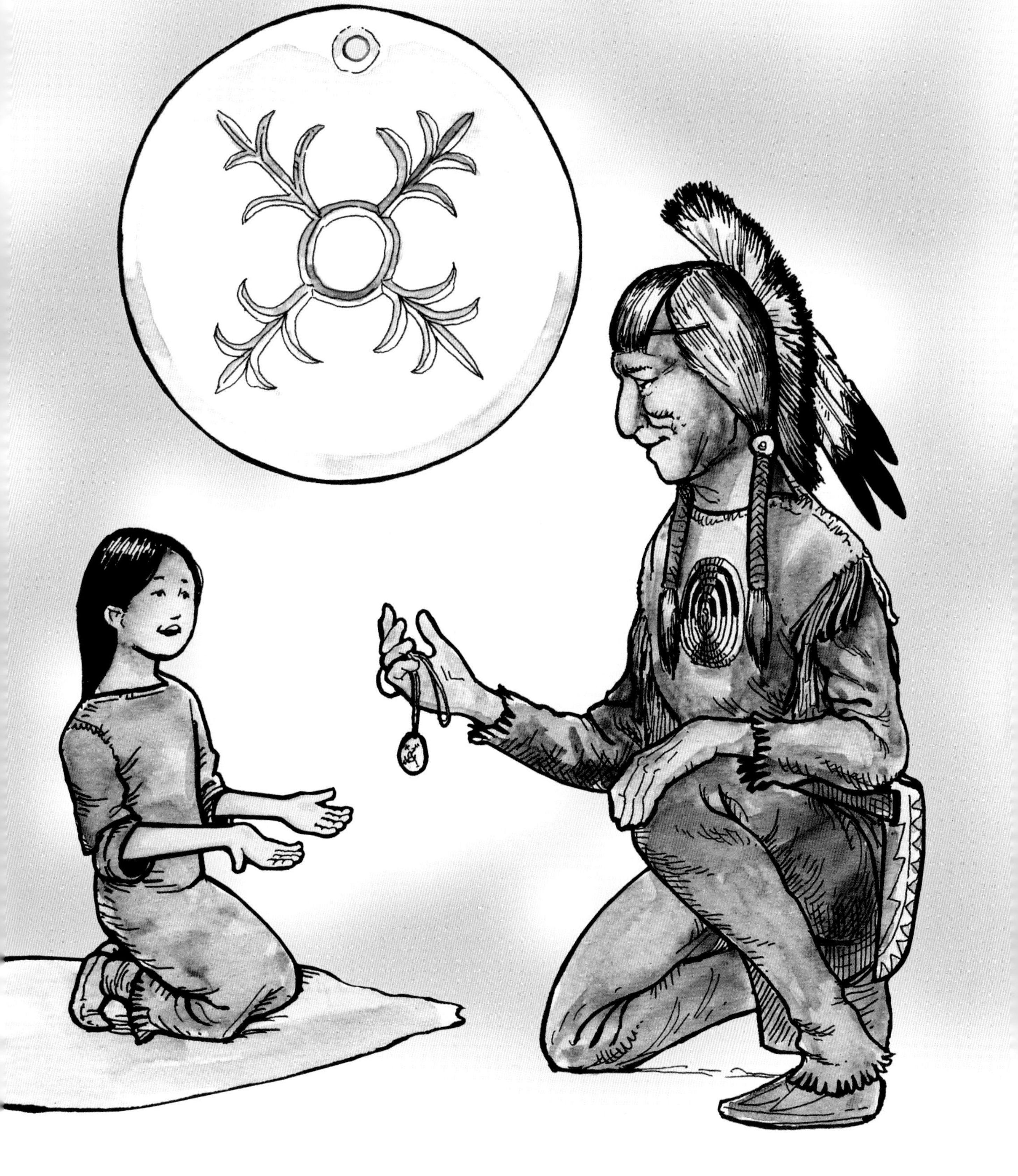

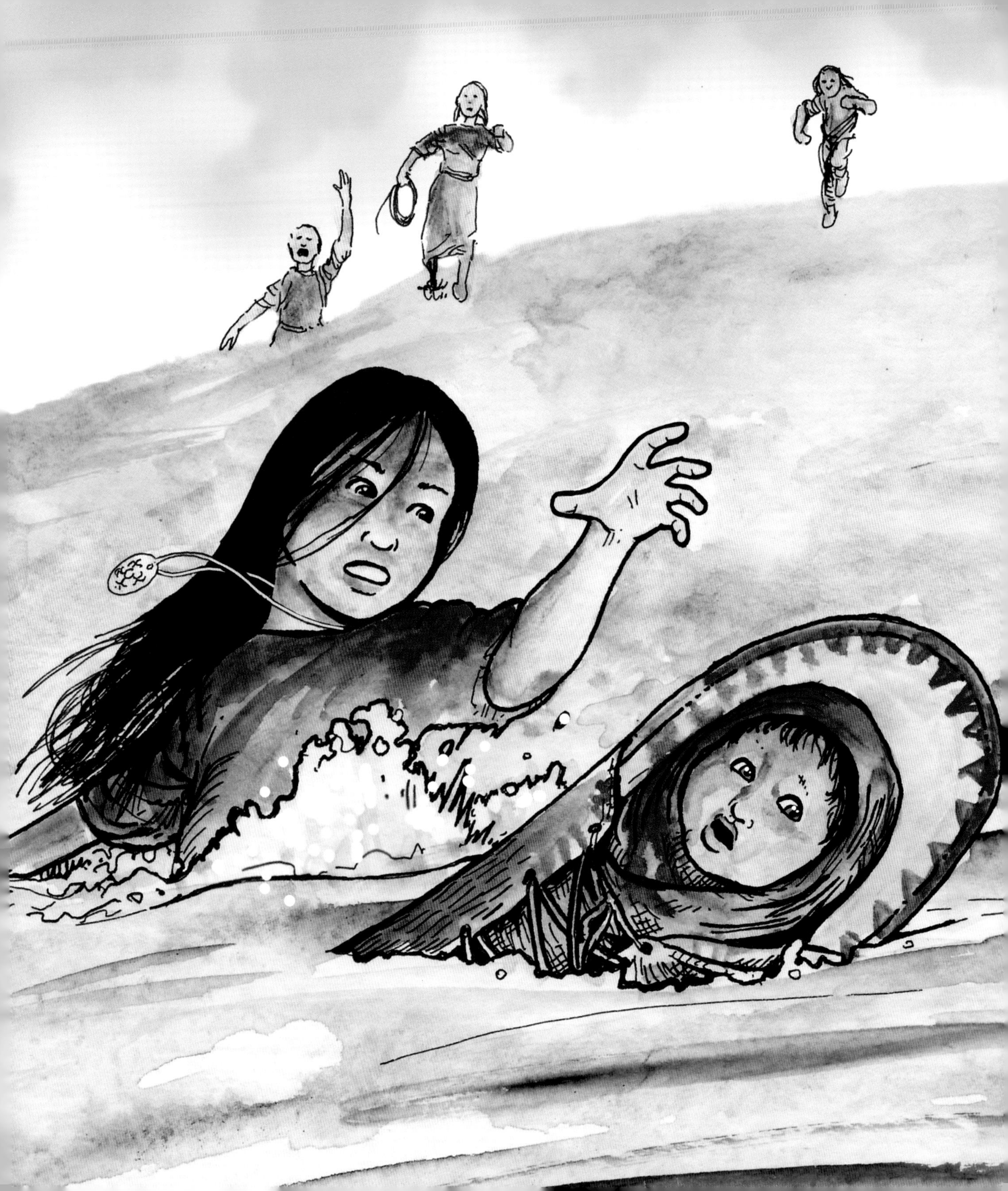

Later that fall, Heron and Muskrat were visiting some cousins camped along a big river. Heron heard frantic screams and looked upriver. A baby, still in its cradle board, came rushing downstream. The child had accidentally fallen into the river.

Without thinking, Heron waded out and grabbed the baby as it raced by. Pulling with all of her might, she wrestled the cradle board to shore.

After much kissing and hugging from the child's mother and relatives, Heron realized that her necklace with the four maize plants was missing. She looked everywhere, but it must have come off in the river.

The fast-flowing Missouri River carried the necklace downstream. It finally came to rest on the river bottom. There it stayed for a long time.

Much changed while the bone carving lay on the river bottom. New people moved into the country. Boats came up and down the river, and bridges spanned the mighty Missouri. Finally, large dams changed the current of the river and set the little amulet free to make its way downstream.

It came to rest on a shoreline in eastern South Dakota. One day, Hannah, a little girl of ten, found it as she walked along the river bank on her grandparents' farm. She picked it up and ran to show her grandfather, who put it on a string for her to wear around her neck.

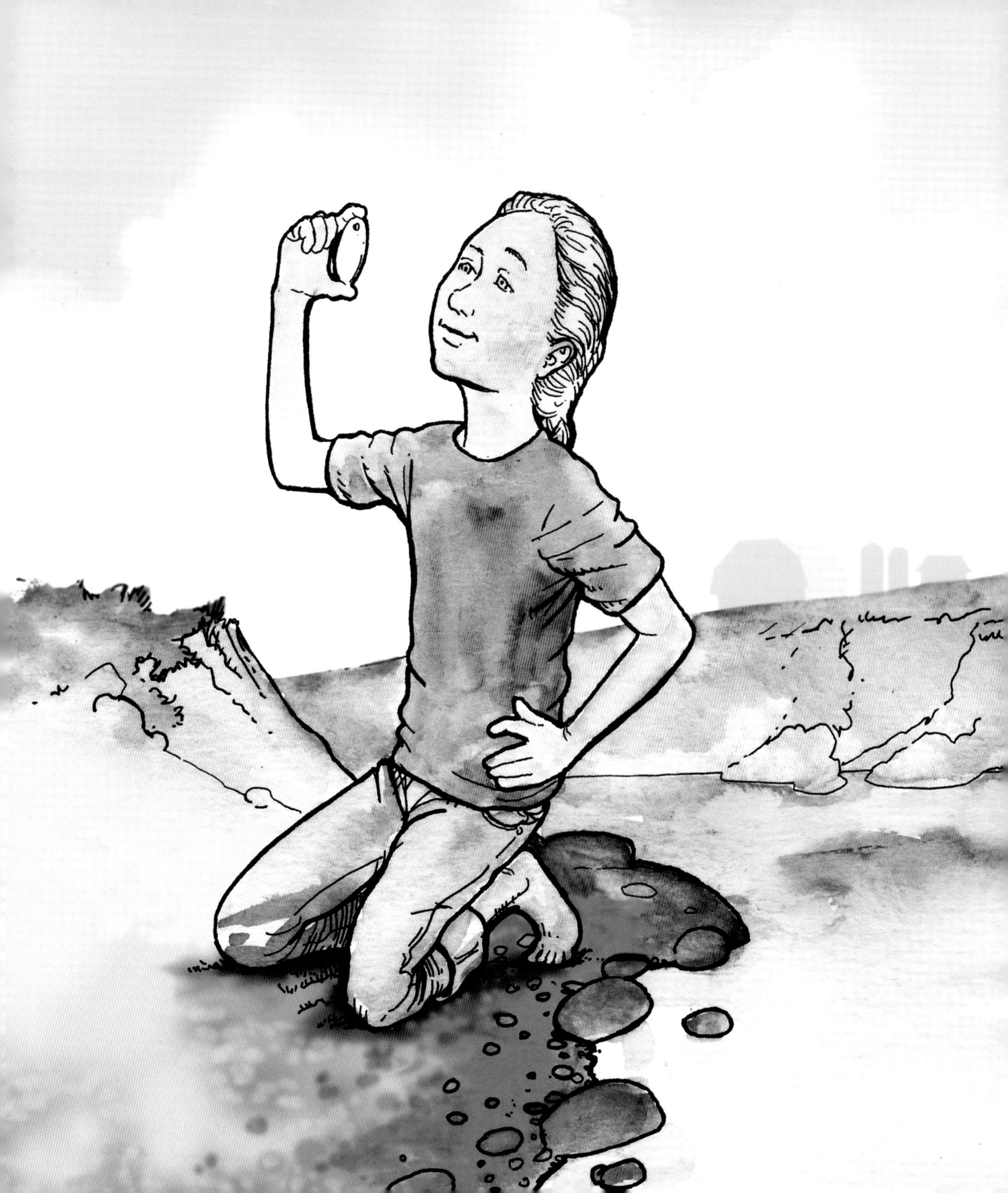

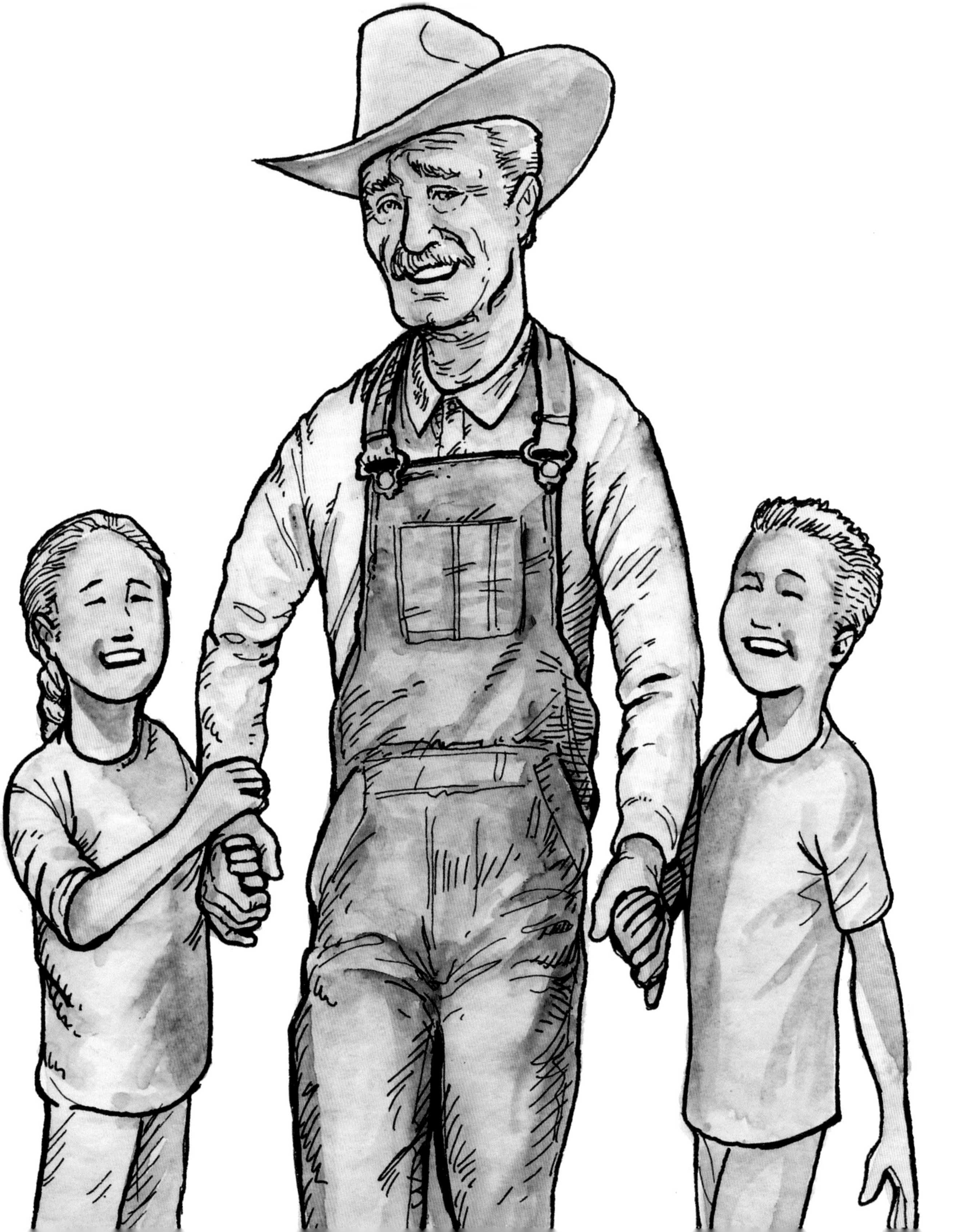

CHAPTER 2

Hannah and Max held their grandfather's large, rough hands and looked up at the huge building. It was covered entirely with corn. An artist and his workers had cut the corn and nailed it onto panels to make pictures. In the hot August sunshine, these murals seemed to shimmer with life.

"It is 'The World's Only Corn Palace,' and it has been in Mitchell, South Dakota, for over one hundred years," Grandpa said. "It was built to celebrate corn and the growing of corn."

Max did not mention that some of his friends called it "The World's Largest Bird Feeder." He knew that his grandfather raised corn on his farm and took his crops seriously.

"Grandpa, do you suppose there is popcorn on this building, and if there is, why doesn't it pop on a hot day like today?" Max asked.

Grandpa laughed. "Max, if you see any popcorn falling off the building, let me know, and I'll run and get us a bowl."

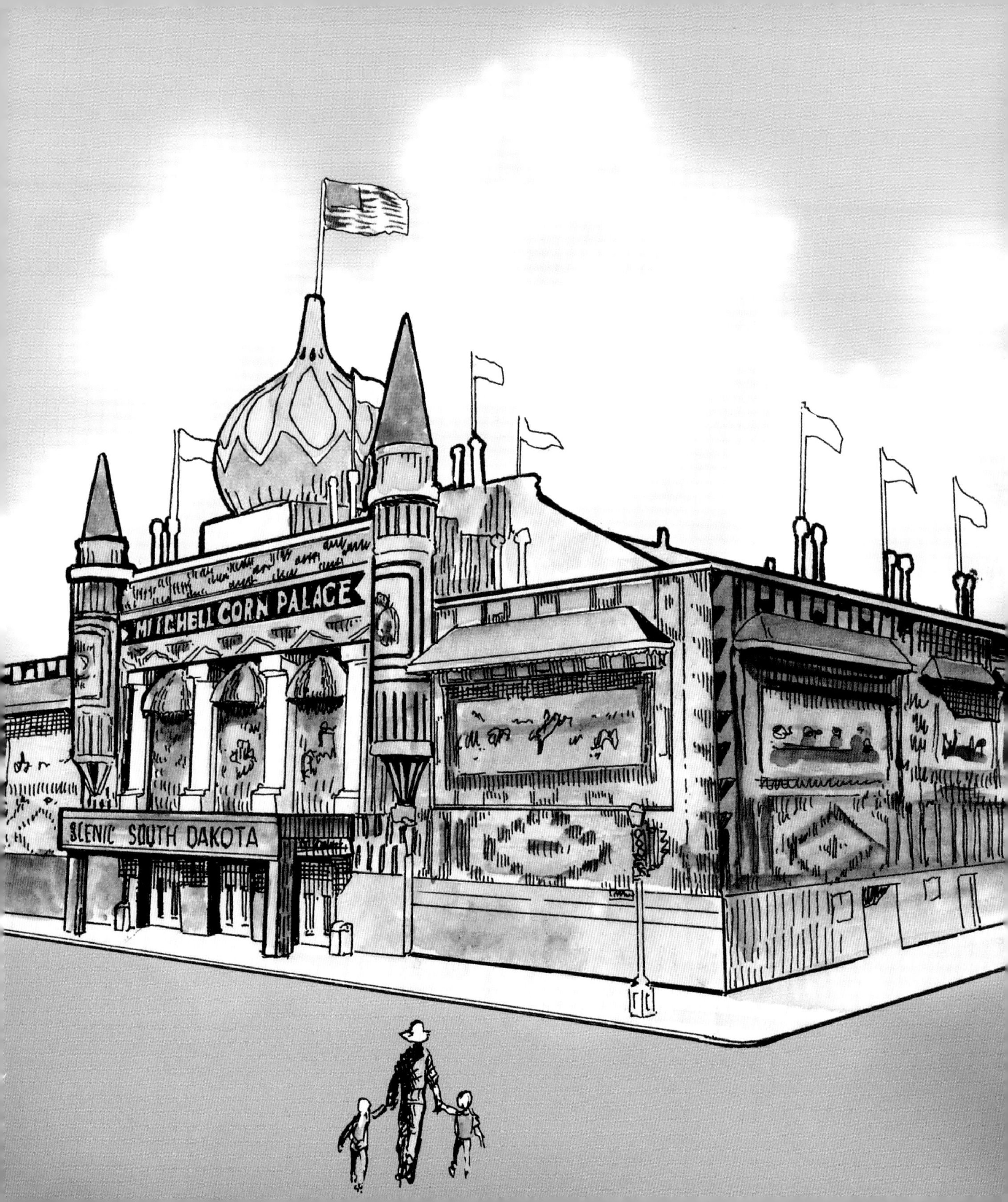
MITCHELL CORN PALACE
SCENIC SOUTH DAKOTA

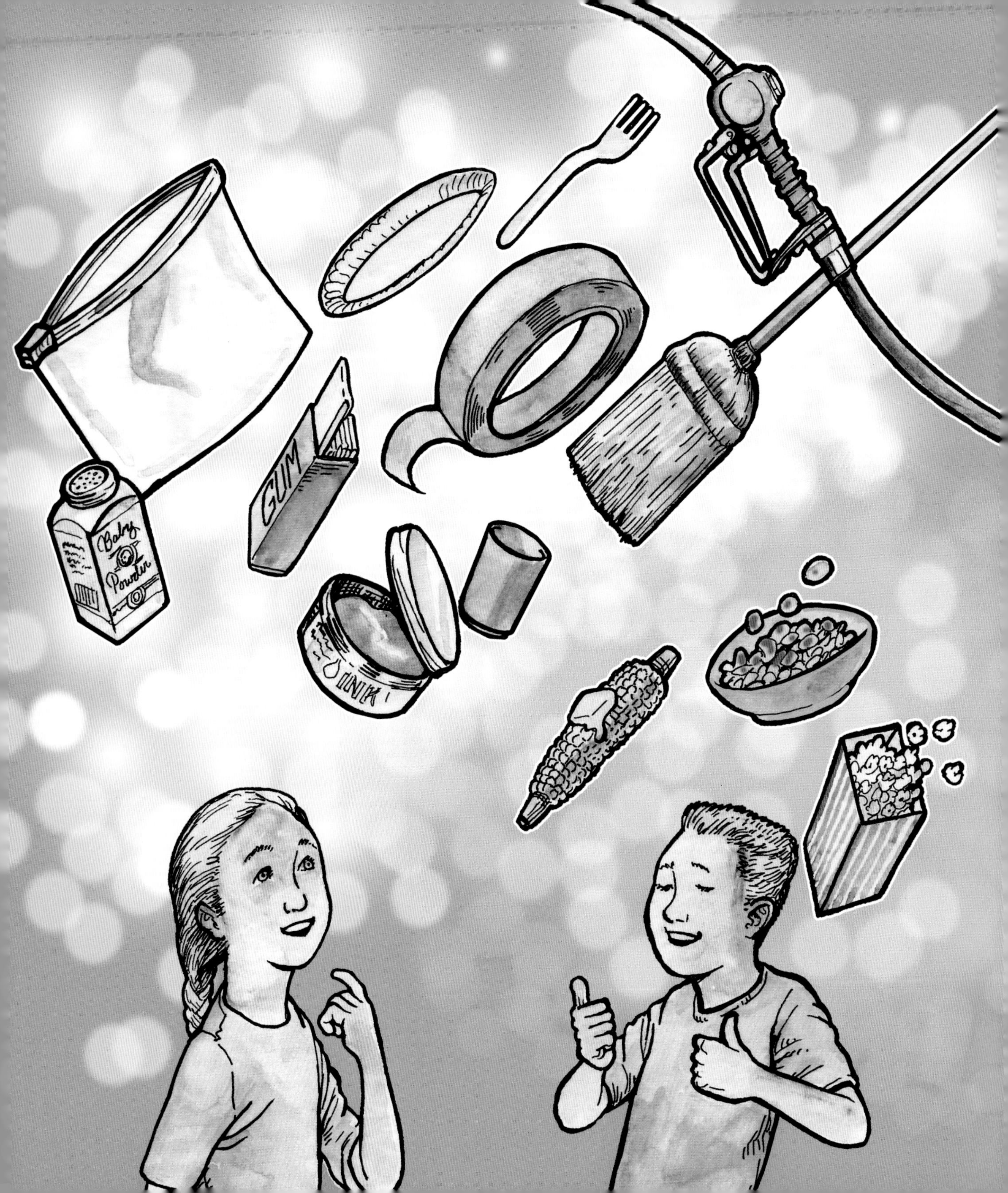
GUM
Baby Powder
INK

Inside, the twins saw more murals created with different colored corn. The biggest surprise came when their guide told them that corn is used to make chewing gum, printing ink, tape, plastic bags, ice cream, fuel for cars—the list went on and on.

To Max and Hannah, corn meant three things: corn flakes for breakfast, sweet corn for dinner in the summer, and Max's favorite, hot, buttered popcorn.

"Corn," the guide said as she led them to a mural, "is also called maize. It was developed in what is now Mexico over seven thousand years ago. Growing corn is what made the large cities of the Aztecs and Mayans possible. It created a stable food supply so that people no longer had to wander in search of food. They could build towns and stay in one place. Through trading, maize slowly made its way to this part of the country."

Hannah and Max were also surprised to learn that people in other parts of the world did not know about corn until the first European explorers brought it back from America over four thousand years ago. Now, corn is grown throughout the world.

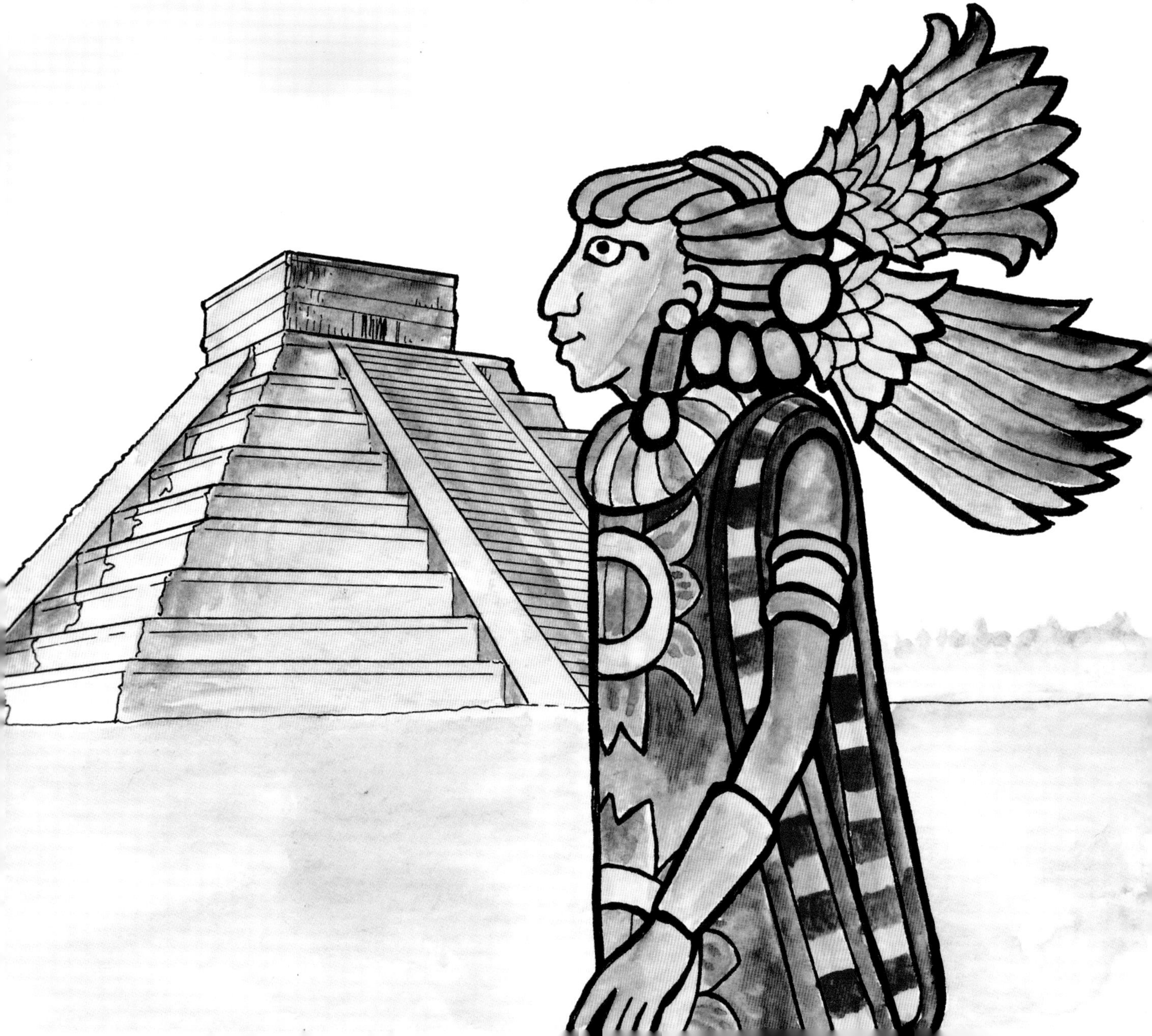

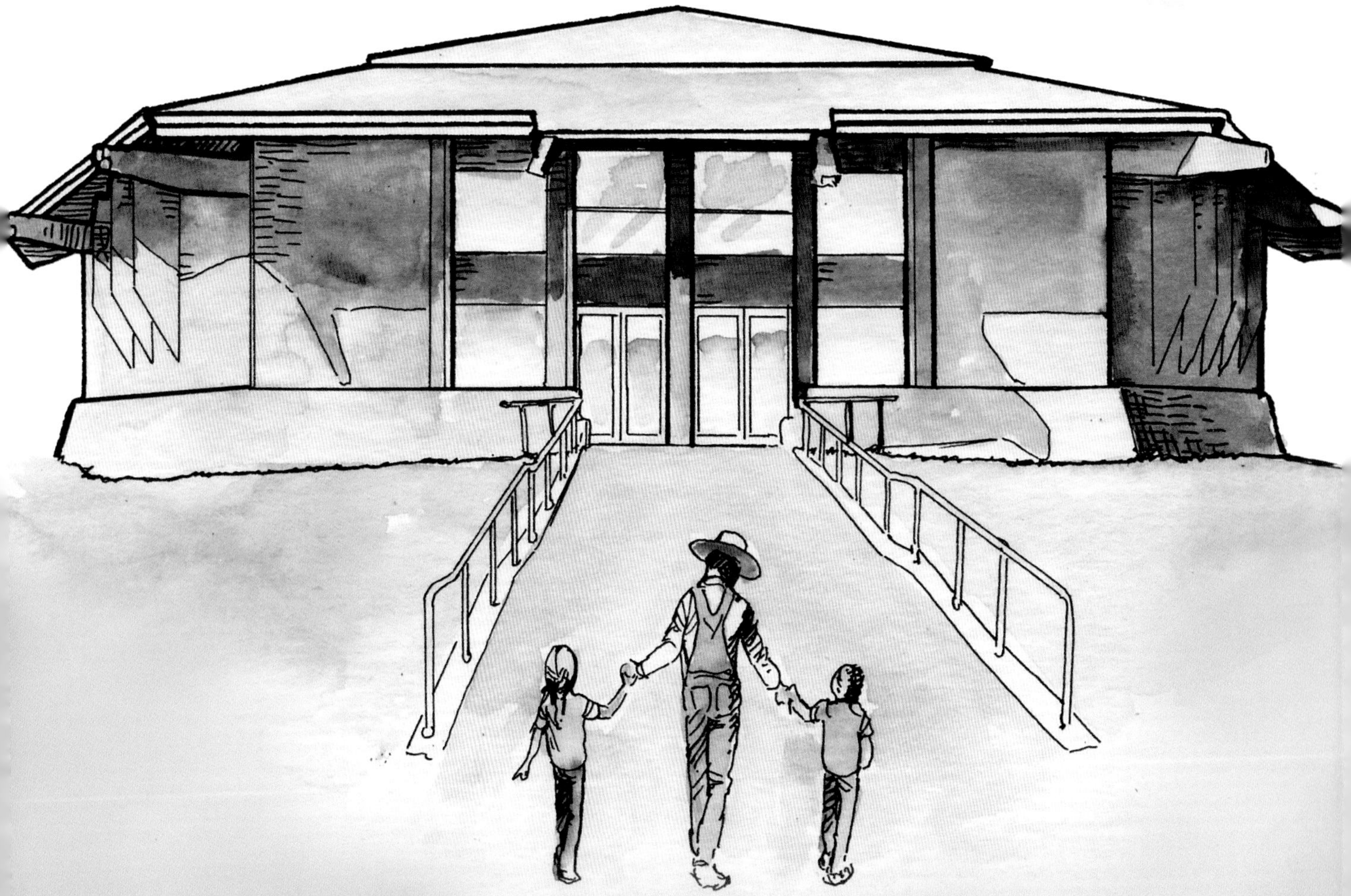

After touring the Corn Palace, the twins climbed into their grandfather's truck. Grandpa put it into gear and turned north toward Lake Mitchell rather than south toward home.

"Grandpa, you're going the wrong way," said Max.

"No, Max," Grandpa said, "we have one more stop on this adventure. We are going to see where this whole corn business began in this part of the world."

A few minutes later, he drove into a parking lot with a sign that read: "Prehistoric Indian Village."

There, next to the lake that used to be a creek, archaeologists were exploring an American Indian village that was over one thousand years old.

Covering the site was a large building called the Archeodome. From a platform around the sides of it, the twins looked down on the site of the village.

Archaeologists worked with small brushes, picks, and trowels, scraping away the earth layer by layer. They carefully sifted through the dirt to find out about people who lived long ago.

Nearby, display cases showed what the archaeologists had uncovered. Seeds found in storage chambers under the ground told the story of what people ate a thousand years ago. Maps and charts told the long history of maize. The twins were surprised when they saw what early corn looked like.

"Grandpa, these ears are awful puny compared to the corn you grow," Max exclaimed as he looked at drawings of the ancient maize.

"It was pretty puny," his grandfather said, "but it was a wonderful discovery, and it changed people's lives."

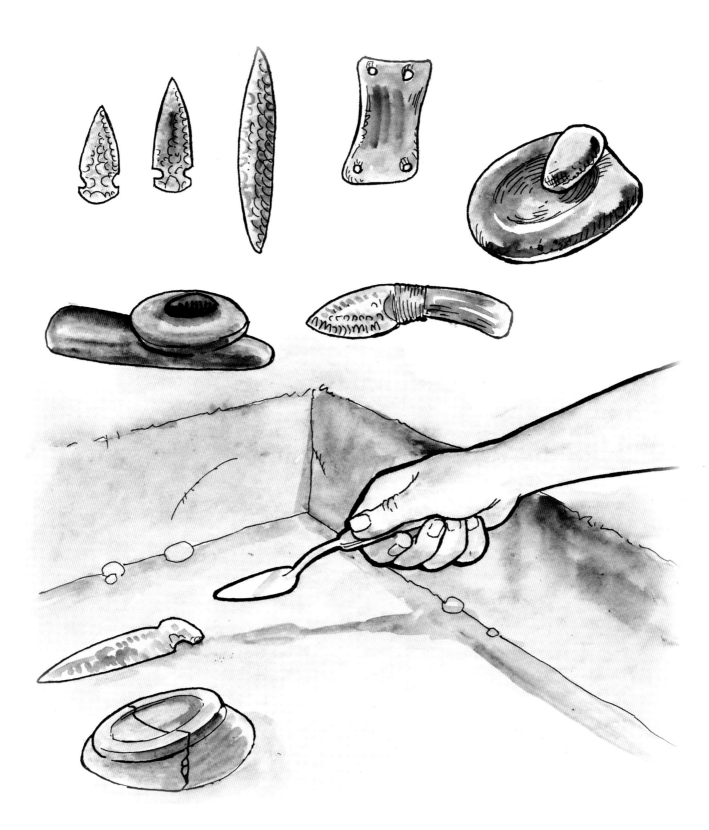

Hannah had grown quiet. She could not understand it, but she felt strange—in a nice sort of way.

While Max was tearing from one exhibit to the next, she walked slowly from case to case. She finally paused in front of one that held personal belongings of the people who had lived on this spot long ago. Inside, she saw a small piece of bone with a carving on it. She reached up and touched the amulet she wore around her neck.

Hannah looked down at the bone necklace with the four maize plants on it. It had always been her special treasure. Now she knew that it was a bond between her and the people who had lived here many years before.

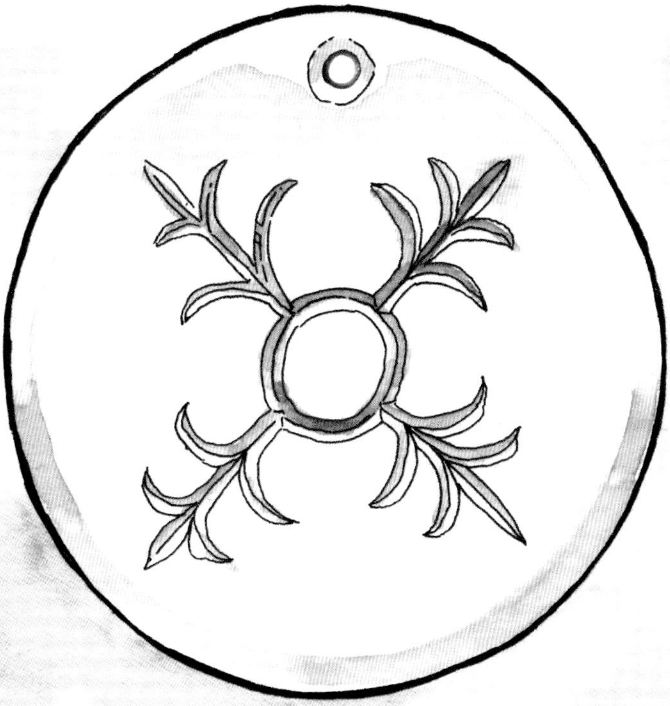

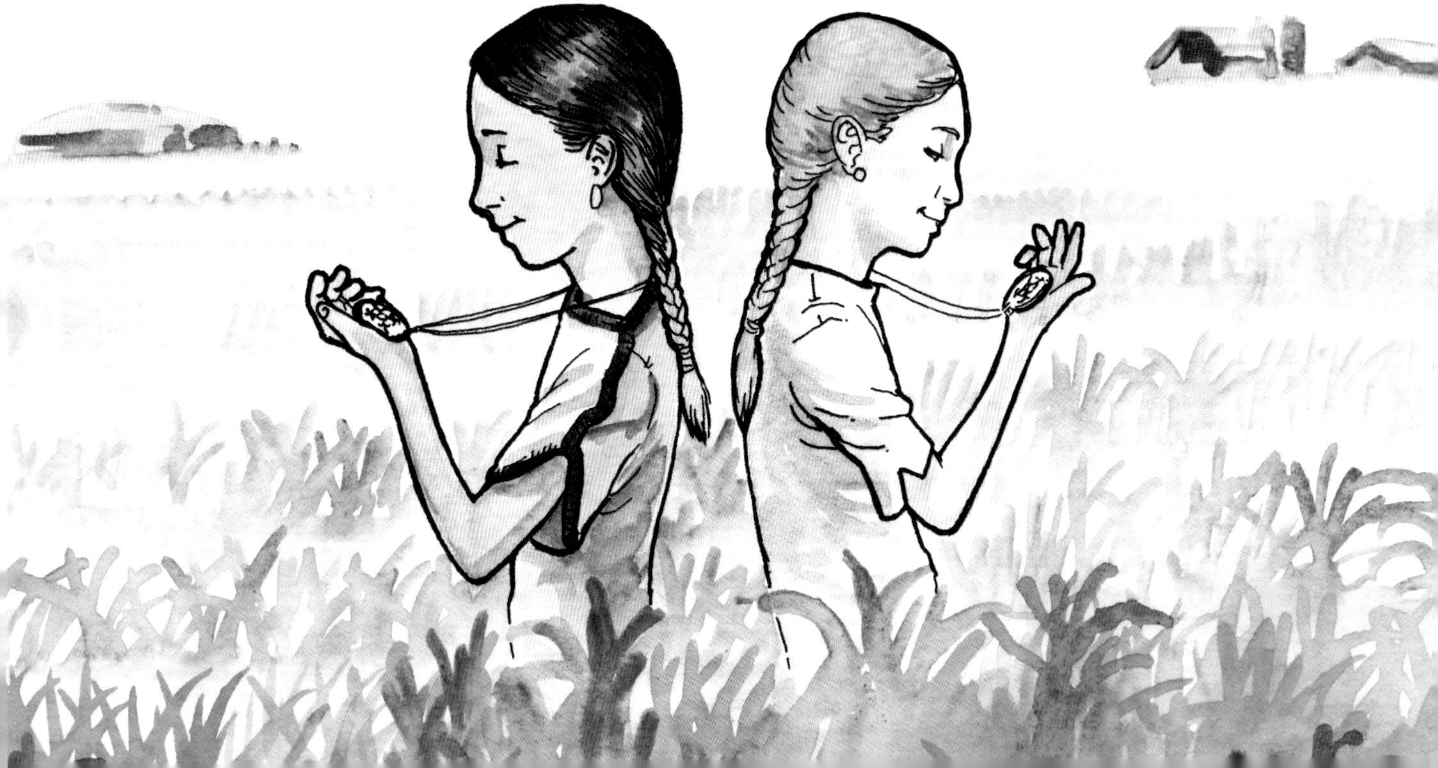

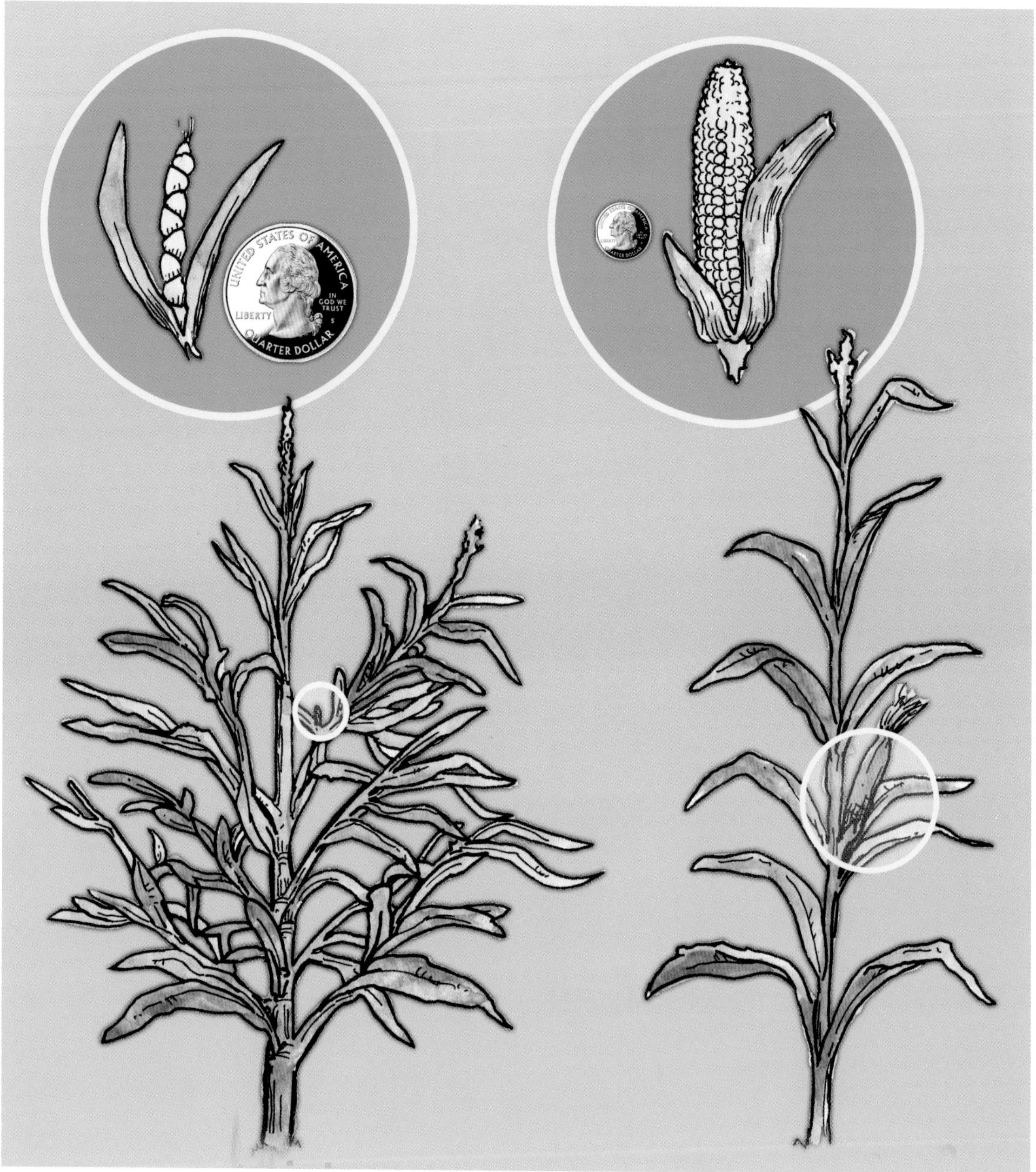
UNITED STATES OF AMERICA
LIBERTY
IN GOD WE TRUST
S
QUARTER DOLLAR

ANCIENT MAIZE

MODERN CORN